SONGS FROM A JOURNEY WITH A PARROT

FROM BRAZIL AND PORTUGAL

Collected by Magdeleine Lerasle
Illustrations by Aurélia Fronty

BOOK 1

1

1 Papagaio loiro

Golden parrot
With the golden beak,
Bring this letter
To my beloved!

He's neither monk,
Nor married,
But young, single,
And as handsome as a carnation!

Papagaio loiro
De bico doirado,
Leva-me esta carta
Ao meu namorado !

Ele não é frade,
Nem homem casado,
É rapaz solteiro
Lindo como um cravo !

2

4

2 O vendedor de água
PORTUGAL

I have water to sell!
Who wants my water?
Cool, cool water!
To refresh my heart!
Buy the water in my jug!
From my jug, from my small goblet,
Little love, buy my water!

Quem compra, compra,
Quem quer comprar,
Água fresquinha pra refrescar,
Pra refrescar meu coração ?
Compra-me a água do garrafão !
Do garrafão, do pucarinho,
Compra-me a água meu amorzinho !

6

3 A janelinha fecha

BRAZIL

The little window closes
When it rains.
The little window opens
When the sun rises.

Closed, open!
Closed, open, closed!

A janelinha fecha
Quando está chovendo.
A janelinha abre
Se o sol está aparecendo.

Fechou, abriu !
Fechou, abriu, fechou !

4 Boi, boi, boi

BRAZIL

Bull, bull, bull,
Bull with the black head,
Take this child,
She's afraid of the mask.

Boi, boi, boi,
Boi da cara preta,
Pega essa menina,
Que tem medo de careta.

8

5 Ó oliveira da serra

PORTUGAL

Mountain olive tree,
The wind carries your flowers.

Ó-li-ó-ai, so sad! No one carries me,
Ó-li-ó-ai, near my love!

Mountain olive tree,
The wind carries your small branches.

Ó-li-ó-ai, so sad! No one carries me,
Ó-li-ó-ai, to my beloved!

Ó oliveira da serra,
O vento leva a flor.

Ó-li-ó-ai, só a mim ninguém me leva,
Ó-li-ó-ai, para o pé do meu amor !

Ó oliveira da serra,
O vento leva a ramada.

Ó-li-ó-ai, só a mim ninguém me leva,
Ó-li-ó-ai, para o pé da minha amada.

9

6 Meu limão, meu limoeiro

BRAZIL

My lemon, my lemon tree,	Meu limão, meu limoeiro,
My jacaranda tree,	Meu pé de jacarandá,
You went past here,	Uma vez esquindô lê lê,
And you went past there,	Outra vez esquindô lá lá,
Oh my brown-haired girl,	Morena, minha morena,
With your vine-like body,	Corpo de linha torcida,
I beg heaven to keep you from being	Queira Deus você não seja
The ruin of my life.	Perdição da minha vida.

10

7 Minhoca, minhoca

BRAZIL

Little earthworm,
Give me a great, big kiss!
— No, no, no, no kisses.
Then I'll steal one!
Smack!

Little earthworm,
You've lost your mind!
Your kiss is wrong,
The mouth is at the other end!
Smack!

Minhoca, minhoca,
Me dá uma beijoca !
– Não dou, não dou, não dou.
Então eu vou roubar !
Smack !

Minhoco, minhoco,
Cê tá ficando louco !
Você beijou errado,
A boca é do outro lado !
Smack !

8 Samba, samba, samba lê lê

BRAZIL

Samba lê lê is sick,
His head is split,
Samba lê lê needs
A good slap.

Samba, samba, samba ô lê lê
Walk on the skirt ruffle, oh la la!

Samba lê lê tá doente,
Tá com a cabeça quebrada,
Samba lê lê precisava
É de uma boa lambada.

Samba, samba, samba ô lê lê
Pisa na barra da saia ô lá lá !

9 Um, dois, feijão com arroz

BRAZIL, PORTUGAL

One, two, beans and rice	Um, dois, feijão com arroz
Three, four, beans on the plate	Três, quatro, feijão no prato
Five, six, custard sauce	Cinco, seis, molhinho inglês
Seven, eight, eat cookies	Sete, oito, comer biscoitos
Nine, ten, eat pastries!	Nove, dez, comer pastéis !

10 De abóbora faz melão

BRAZIL

From a pumpkin, make us a melon
From a melon, make us a watermelon
Make us some sweets, sinhá, make us candied fruit
Make us maracujá* jam
Those who wish to learn to dance
Go to Juquinha's house.

He leaps, he dances
And oh, how he sways!

* Maracujá: A variety of passion fruit.

De abóbora faz melão
De melão faz melancia
Faz doce, sinhá, faz doce sinhá
Faz doce de maracujá
Quem quiser aprender a dançar
Vai à casa do Juquinha.

Ele pula, ele dança
Ele faz requebradinha

11 Se essa rua fosse minha

BRAZIL

If this street, if this street were mine,
I would, I would pave it
With precious stones, brilliant sparkles,
For my love, my love to walk down.

On this street, on this street there is a wood
That is called, that is called solitude
In that wood, in that wood lives an angel
Who stole, who stole my heart.

If I stole, if I stole, I stole your heart,
You stole, you stole mine as well.
If I stole, if I stole, I stole your heart,
It's because, it's because I love you so.

Se essa rua, se essa rua fosse minha,
Eu mandava, eu mandava ladrilhar
Com pedrinhas, com pedrinhas de brillantes,
Para o meu, para o meu amor passar.

Nessa rua, nessa rua tem um bosque
Que se chama, que se chama solidão.
Dentro dele, dentro dele mora um anjo
Que roubou, que roubou meu coração.

Se eu roubei, se eu roubei teu coração,
Tu roubaste, tu roubaste o meu também.
Se eu roubei, se eu roubei teu coração,
É porque, é porque te quero bem.

12 Dedo mindinho

PORTUGAL

Here's a riddle!	Éste é um conto de adivinha !
Here's the little one (the little finger)	Dedo mindinho
Here's the little bird (the ring finger)	O passarinho
Here's the largest of all (the middle finger)	O maior de todos
Here's the cake decorator (the index finger)	O pinta bolos
Here's the flea killer (the thumb)	O mata piolhos
Trick!	Tric !

13 Tão balalão

PORTUGAL

Tan balalan! A dog's head!	Tão balalão, cabeça de cão !
Cat's ears and no heart!	Orelhas de gato, não tem coração !
Tan balalan! Simon is dead!	Tão balalão, morreu o Simão !
In land of the Moors, Captain Sir!	Na terra dos Mouros, Senhor capitão !
Tan balalan! A dog's head!	Tão balalão, cabeça de cão !
Cooked and roasted in my kettle!	Cozida e assada no meu caldeirão !

14 Escravos de Jó

BRAZIL

Job's slaves
Pretended to be crabs.
Take, place,
Spin the zambele!*

From warrior to warrior,
We go zig, zig, zag!

* Zambele: A small object that
  can be used for percussion.
  Also the name of a nocturnal bird.

Escravos de Jó
Jogavam caxangá.
Tira, bota,
Deixa o zambele ficar !

Guerreiros com guerreiros
Fazem zig, zig, zá !

15 Fui no Itororó

BRAZIL

I went to Itororó
To drink water, but I couldn't find it.
I found a beautiful girl
But left her behind, in Itororó.

Friends, enjoy life now!
One night is nothing at all.
If we don't sleep now,
We'll sleep at dawn.

Oh! Dona Maria, oh! Little Maria,
Enter the circle or you'll be all alone!
— All alone, not I, no, never shall I be!
Because Chico is my partner!

Lift your little foot,
Place it next to mine,
But don't you later say,
You wish you never had!

Fui no Itororó
Beber água e não achei.
Só achei bela morena
Que no Itororó deixei.

Aproveite minha gente
Que uma noite não é nada.
Se não dormir agora,
Dormirá de madrugada.

Oh ! Dona Maria, oh ! Mariazinha,
Entra nesta roda ou ficarás sózinha
– Sózinha eu não fico nem hei-de ficar !
Pois tenho o Chico para ser meu par !

Tira o seu pezinho,
Bota ao pé do meu,
E depois não diga,
Que se arrependeu !

22

ABOUT THE SONGS

Who remembers when Portugal's Indian Armada set out on March 15, 1500,
to conquer the New World? All the bells in Lisbon rang "Tão balalão" to honour the
event. The 15 nursery rhymes and songs from Brazil and Portugal selected for this
album–out of the more than 300 that were collected–underscore both the individuality
of these two countries and the bonds that unite them beyond their common language.

In Brazil, although popular traditional children's music is European in origin
(primarily French and Portuguese, as well as Italian, Dutch and Spanish),
it also draws on African and Native American traditions–as shown
in "Escravos de Jó" or "Boi, boi, boi".

In Portugal, the repertory of music often carries us back to a time in the past when life
was regulated by sowing and harvesting, the flow of the seasons, religious festivals
and so on. Yet, today, Portuguese children continue to sing "As pombinhas da Cat'rina".
Do Portuguese children realize that, on the other side of the Atlantic, the melodies of
many songs they sing also ring out in Brazilian schoolyards?

In fact, traditional children's songs travel from Lisbon to Bahia and from Porto to Rio.
And, while it is difficult to define this changing corpus, such songs help to maintain
the deep connection between the two countries.

1 Papagaio loiro (Golden Parrot)

BRAZIL, PORTUGAL
Singer Ariane Badie

This rhyming song is sung to children, but like many others, it derives from a love song. In the original version, the young girl asks a parrot to carry a letter to her beloved, who has gone "to the other side of the ocean, to the other shore" (*para o outro lado, para a outra margem*). She compares him to a carnation, a common flower in Portugal, and a symbol of beauty and elegance. For example, to express admiration, people will say, "*Você cheira a cravo* " (You smell like a carnation). Long unknown to Europeans, then brought over from Brazil by the caravels, the parrot became a mythical bird in Portugal.

Moreover, in chronicles written by French author Abbé de Raynal at the end of the 18th century, he mentions the banished and the expatriates, who apparently used these *papagaios* to send news to their relatives in Europe: "Every year, two ships set out from Portugal, carrying all the criminals, the deportees, the banished and the fallen women to the New World… They came back laden with parrots and precious wood…" It is amusing to note that the parrot says *lóro, lóro* in Brazil and *cro, cro* in Portugal. On the recording, the musician plays the bandolim, an eight-stringed instrument of the mandolin family.

2 O vendedor de água (The Water Seller)

PORTUGAL
Singers Alice Machado, Irène Machado

24

This work song evokes the traditional figure of the Madeira water seller, walking up and down the sunny streets of Funchal, calling out to passers-by by clinking his pewter goblet against the clay jar or the straw-covered jug carried on his back. In Portugal, in the era of steam trains, water-sellers could also be seen on platforms of overheated stations. The music cheerfully combines accordion, percussion and guitar. There is also another series of lines that is not part of the recording:

Quem quer comprar que eu vendo?
Eu preciso de vender uma casa sem telhado
E com as paredes por fazer!

Who wants to buy what I have to sell?
What I have to sell, is a house with no roof
With walls that still have to be built!

3 A janelinha fecha (The Little Window Closes)

BRAZIL

Singers Ophélie Dorn, Amélie Maillot, Cindy Ramos, Marine Rossignol

In every language, simple word games paired with actions like caressing and tickling help children develop an awareness of their face and body. Such games are often played at bath time. In this song, eyes are compared to small windows that open and close, depending on the weather. The comparison is also a good way to familiarize young children with notions of presence and absence, and to develop a nurturing relationship of tender encouragement between mother and child. This song shares similarities with *Xi coração* , a well-known nursery rhyme in Portugal, in which the adult stretches out their arms to a child and covers them with kisses:

Xi coração, aperta amor, dei um abraço, numa linda flor!
Come, my sweetheart, hold me tight, I've kissed a pretty flower!

4 Boi, boi, boi (Bull, Bull, Bull)

BRAZIL

Singers Alice Machado, Irène Machado, Ophélie Dorn, Amélie Maillot, Cindy Ramos, Marine Rossignol

This very old and mysterious lullaby, by an unknown author, is certainly the best known in Brazil. On the recording, it is presented first in its traditional form, whispered into someone's ear. In the following version, the lullaby is transformed by the young singers into a wild samba, with a rhythm defined by the batucada style of percussion, which uses a mix of drums (*cuica, surdo, tamborim, repinique, caixa*), whistles (*apito*), gourds (*reco-reco*), rattles (*caxixi*) and iron bells (*agogo*). The strange lyrics inspire fear in children. In Brazil, a bull with a black head (*boi da cara preta*) is the equivalent of the boogeyman. When children misbehave, parents threaten to call the bull, pointing to a dark room in the depths of the house. Although children soon learn that the bull does not exist, they pretend to be afraid.

5 Ó oliveira da serra (Mountain Olive Tree)

PORTUGAL
Singers Alice Machado, Irène Machado

This work song belongs to the tradition of harvest and romance songs (*cantigas de serga e romance*), much like the famous "Ó alecrim". In the hearts of the Portuguese, both songs represent their homeland. Traditionally, these call-and-response songs were used by harvesters to keep the pace and help them forget their fatigue. They most likely share a lineage with *Os Lusiadas* , an epic verse by Luis Vaz de Camões, which is evident through the way they transform daily activities into poetic rhymes and express themes of love and freedom. Today, these songs are taught in schools and choral groups, and often sung during popular festivals.

6 Meu limão, meu limoeiro (My Lemon, My Lemon Tree)

BRAZIL
Singer Gerson Leonardi

This gentle, melodious *samba-canção* , which children dance to by swaying and sliding their feet from side to side, is a true love song. In the popular symbolism of Bahia, the *jacaranda* –a rare and valuable tree–refers to a woman of mixed ancestry, an idealized image of feminine beauty and sensuality, whose supple, bronzed body is associated with images of slender branches or wisps of cigar smoke. Similarly, the lemon tree, which changes appearance and colour with the wind, may be associated with the versatility of womanhood. On the recording, the song is performed by a male singer accompanied by accordion, guitar, bass, maracas and cuica in a bossa nova rhythm.

7 Minhoca, minhoca (Little Earthworm)

BRAZIL
Singers **Ophélie Dorn, Amélie Maillot, Cindy Ramos, Marine Rossignol**

This type of tickling game is played around the world. The animal used in this game really depends on the country it's played in. In France, it's a creepy crawler that climbs up and up; in the Maghreb, an ant or small mouse; in Portugal or Brazil, a cat and mouse that chase one another. In this case, the mother imitates an earthworm that crawls over the baby's body, stopping at three precise points (tummy, bottom, feet). Finally, the earthworm plants a big, noisy kiss on an unexpected spot. On the recording, the children's voices are backed by the *reco-reco*, a gourd that is played by scraping its ridges with a stick.

8 Samba, samba, samba lê lê

BRAZIL
Singers **Gerson Leonardi, Ophélie Dorn, Amélie Maillot, Cindy Ramos, Marine Rossignol**

Known throughout the world, this children's song is a samba, a popular dance with strong African influences that's synonymous with carnival festivities. In Brazil, the samba is a way of life, like a religion that assumes its full importance during carnival. It exemplifies how cultures and traditions have blended in Brazil, allowing Brazilians of African origins to preserve and fuse their religion and dance traditions, such as the rituals of *candomblé*. In this song, *Samba lê lê* is a clumsy young boy who steps on his partner's skirt and receives a good slap (*uma boa lambada*) in return. Children adore singing and miming this song. The recording starts with a long *maracatu* (a rhythm from the northeast region), after which the accordion develops the melodic line.

27

9 Um, dois, feijão com arroz (One, Two, Beans and Rice)

BRAZIL, PORTUGAL
Singer Fabien Lopes

While this counting and elimination song is also known in Portugal, it is much more popular in Brazil. The *feijão* (a small black bean) is both the basic ingredient in *feijoada*, Brazil's national dish, and a symbol of economic power: the equivalent of "daily bread." On the recording, a boy's chanting voice is backed by a *batucada* drumming ensemble. *Batucada* drumming can even be improvised with two coffee spoons, a box of matches, a frying pan and other items on hand.

10 De abóbora faz melão (From a Pumpkin Make Us a Melon)

BRAZIL
Singers Ophélie Dorn, Amélie Maillot,
Cindy Ramos, Marine Rossignol

This circle dance, which is mimed and sung, harkens back to colonial Brazil, a time when social order was organized around the production of sugar. On one side, there is the imposing and austere house of the boss, where his wife (*la sinhá*) was confined. On the other, there is the dwelling for enslaved people (represented by the casa do *Juquinha*), where people danced and sang. Children adore this song, which lists the fruits of Brazil and the sweets of days gone by: *papos de anjos, cabelos de anjos, doce de maracujá, bananada* and *cocada*. They dance, jump and swing their hips to light, lively music that combines European and Afro-Brazilian instruments like the accordion bells, guitar and maracas.

11 Se essa rua fosse minha (If This Street Were Mine)

BRAZIL
Singer Gerson Leonardi

This very poetic *modinha* (traditional love song) evokes the absence of the beloved in a melancholic manner. The modinha, which first appeared in the Brazilian colony and was then performed for court soirées in Lisbon at the end of the 18ᵗʰ century, remains a vibrant and popular genre in Brazil. This version may have been sung by miners after a hard day at work looking for gold and precious stones in Ouro Preto, Congonhia, Mariana or Diamantina.

12 Dedo mindinho (Here's The Little One)

PORTUGAL
Singer Filismena Correia

This finger game, from Portugal's Serra da Estrela region, is a veritable piece of theatre used to distract or calm a crying baby. As the curtain rises, the adult makes an emphatic announcement. The most common is *Éste é um conto de adivinha* (Here's a riddle). Then, the adult recites the rhyme, grabbing each of the child's fingers and shaking them. There are many variations which often depend on the mood or the memory of the person reciting them. The cake decorator is, of course, the index finger of an impatient, greedy child who dips his finger in the batter. The final action, which the child waits for in excitement, evokes the sound of fingernails breaking loose eggs!

This type of codified finger game, which is often followed by tickling, is very widespread in the Mediterranean world. It can be compared to the Brazilian rhyme "Cade o toucinho que estava aqui" ("Where is the piece of lard that was here?"), a riddle and addition song imported from Portugal.

13 Tão balalão (Ding Ding Dong)

PORTUGAL
Singer Ana-Rita Perreira

In this swinging game, a child is seated on an adult's knees. The adult holds them by the hands and swings them back and forth in a rhythm that evokes church bells. "Tão balalão" brings to mind the sound of the powerful bell that announces important events: birth, the death of a loved one or the passing of a well-known person. The song is also a nursery rhyme used to scare children. One can only imagine the frightening character it describes. Not so long ago, people still threatened children who were acting up by saying: "Be careful, or the Moors will come and get you!"–a historical reference to the Moorish occupation of Portugal.

14 Escravos de Jó (Job's Slaves)

BRAZIL
Singers Ophélie Dorn, Amélie Maillot,
Cindy Ramos, Marine Rossignol

All Brazilian children have played "Escravos de Jó" at one time or another, and all adults recall such play with nostalgia. The game involves percussion and skill. Children sit in a circle, with one or two objects placed in front of them (preferably objects that make sounds, such as a box of matches or shells). When the song starts, they grab the object and pass it from hand to hand, crossing and uncrossing their arms in keeping with the rhythm and the words. The back-and-forth, coming-and-going movement to *zig, zig, zá* evokes the sidewise walk of crabs and their battling claws. When someone makes a mistake and breaks the rhythm, they are eliminated.

The *caxanga*, a synonym of *siripu*, is a swamp crab that gives its name to a type of *capoeira*, a choreographic martial art of Bantu origin, developed to some degree in Bahia. Occasionally, children play while standing close behind one another; they form a closed circle and move the object ahead, arms held down, without seeing it. Influenced by candomblé rituals, the typical Afro-Brazilian musical arrangement combines the *pandeiro, atabaque,* bells made of shells, *ganzá*s, flute and *agogo*.

15 Fui no Itororó (I Went To Itororó)

BRAZIL
Singer Gerson Leonardi

This circle dance is suitable for complex and amusing movements, for both groups and individuals. Children skip in a circle until the child designated as Dona Maria enters the middle and walks in the opposite direction. She chooses a partner and they both start the foot game. The children in the larger circle play as well, in twos. Each moves their foot forward to touch their partner's while maintaining balance and rhythm: right foot with right foot, left foot with left foot. Then the circle dance starts again. Games of courtship around wells and fountains form the basis for this very rich repertoire of music. In this case, the story is about an amorous meeting at the Itororó fountain (a name that means "singing stone" in Tupi-guarani) and its origins can be clearly traced to medieval Iberian tradition.

Song selection, notes and vocal coordination Magdeleine Lerasle Illustrations Aurélia Fronty
Record Producer Paul Mindy Musical arrangement Jean-Christophe Hoarau and Paul Mindy
Vocal direction Gerson Leonardi Musicians Christian Toucas (accordion), Tarcisio Pinto Gondim (guitars,
cavaquinho and bandolim), Paul Mindy (percussion) and Jean-Christophe Hoarau (guitar, cavaquinho, bass
and synthesizer) Recorded by Jean-Christophe Hoarau Mixed and mastered by Philippe Kadosch
at Multicrea Graphic Design Stephan Lorti for Haus Design and Isabelle Southgate Translation from
Portuguese to French Alice Machado Translation from French to English Tim Brierly and Sheryl Curtis
for Les Services d'édition Guy Connolly Copy editing Ruth Joseph and Katie Sehl Proofreading Paula Gouveia

Acknowledgments

Augusts Feirrera, Jean-François and Vincent Lerasle, Marie-Claire Glain, Claudine Napp, Maryvonne Lafont,
Teresa Soares, Teresa and Daniela Cerdeira, Paulo Da Cruz, Alice and Dona Flor Ramos, Palmira Arraujo, Lucia
and Carlos Arraujo, Marie-Claire Château, Sonia Andrade, Maria Gonçalves, Isabel Minhos,
Aline Barbosa, Isabelle Lafon.

This work was published with the support of the Institut français' grant program.
Cet ouvrage a bénéficié du soutien du Programme d'aide à la publication de l'Institut français.